KT-116-898

EGMONT

We bring stories to life

First published in Great Britain in 2014
by Egmont UK Limited,
The Yellow Building, 1 Nicholas Road, London W11 4AN

Edited by Frank Tennyson. Designed by Iain Fryer and Mauricio Beltran. Written by Nick Watkins and Richard Jenkins.
Further editing by Simon Ward and Phil Boucher. Cartoon strips by Russ Carvell and Lew Stringer. Pictures: Paul Ashman

ISBN 978 1 4052 7211 7
57518/1
Printed in Italy

Stay safe online. Any website addresses listed in this book are correct at the time of going to print. However, Egmont is not
responsible for content hosted by third parties. Please be aware that online content can be subject to change and websites
can contain content that is unsuitable for children. We advise that all children are supervised when using the internet.
Adult supervision is recommended when glue, paint, scissors and other sharp points are in use.

WELCOME TO

TOXIC

DEAR READER

We've gathered the best moments from our awesome **TOXIC MAGAZINE** and put them together in one very special place! So fasten your seat belts and prepare your laughing gear for take off!

Team Toxic

TOXIC

THIS ANNUAL BELONGS TO ...

----

www.toxicmag.co.uk

CONTENTS

MARIO!

MINIONS!

SKYLANDERS!

TEAM TOXIC IN DOUBLE DANGER! PART 1

ARE YOU THE SORT OF KID WHO PICKS HIS NOSE AND FLIPS THE BOGIES AWAY?

WELL HERE'S WHAT HAPPENS WHEN YOU **DO**!

FLIP!

THE EVIL TECHNO TROLL GRABS THEM ALL UP!

GRAB!

AND TAKES THEM DOWN TO HIS **UNDERGROUND** HIDEOUT!

ALRIGHT, CAPTION WRITER! YOU DON'T NEED TO EXPLAIN **EVERY** MOVE I MAKE!

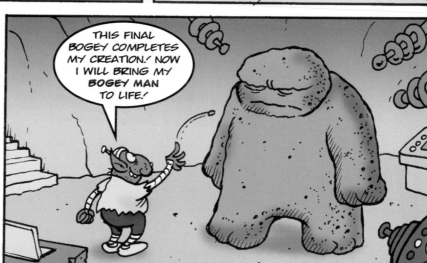

THIS FINAL BOGEY COMPLETES MY CREATION! NOW I WILL BRING MY BOGEY MAN TO LIFE!

ZZAP!

URRGH! WHAT IS YOUR COMMAND, MY BIG-NOSED MASTER?

LESS OF YOUR CHEEK FOR A START! NOW, GO TO THE SURFACE WORLD AND **DESTROY**! HAHAHA!

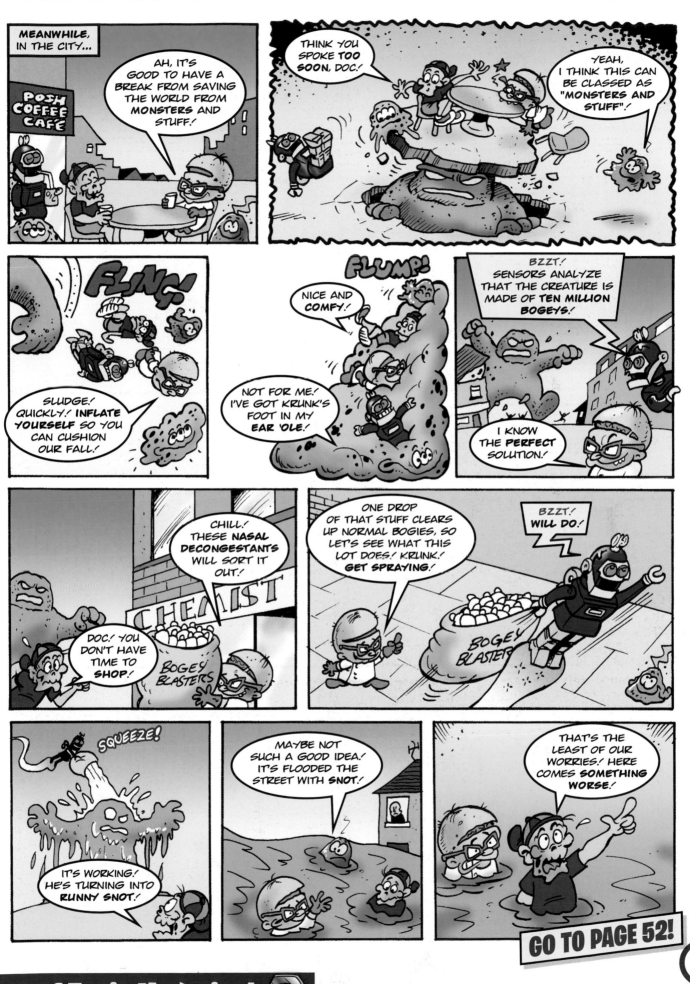

THE WORLD'S BIGGEST...
SEAL!
BLUBBER BOY!
This southern elephant seal is taller than a Polar Bear. He also tucks into around 9kgs of fish every day and weighs in at a whopping 4,000kgs! That's about the same as 10,724 unopened cans of fizzy pop. Mental!
PAH! THIS WON'T FILL ME UP!
HOPE YOU'RE HUNGRY!
Picture: EPA/Corbis

DRAW A MINION!

Sketch your favourite mini-henchman!

DRAW HERE!

JUST FOR FUN!

TEE, HEE SMELL MY FINGER!

Jot down your fave Despicable Me character – or even create one of your own!

It takes a very brave, or very silly man, to get this close! This 18-foot-long shark isn't dangerous according to diver and photographer Daniel Botelho. Er, we'll take your word for that mate!

Picture: Barcroft Media

INVASION!
Where weird worlds collide!

WHAT TO DO!

Captain Gross has invaded Mario Kart land. But like all top superheroes, he's made himself tricky to find! Can you locate all 10 mini-Captain Gross images before the karts spin out on a puddle of sticky snot?

FIND ME!

JUST FOR FUN!

24

LOL!
FUNNIEST PIX YOU'LL EVER SEE!

I SHOULD BE IN THE AVENGERS!

BEAR FRUIT!

After running around scaring people in Colorado, USA, Boulder the Black Bear fell out of a tree! But it's OK - he was tranquilised by wildlife officers before falling onto a crash mat. So he wasn't hurt at all. PHEW!

Picture: PA Images

when animals LOL!

These crazy creatures love nothing better than a good old giggle!

WHAT'S SO FUNNY?

MAD MONKEY ⬣
Has someone told this guy he's been given a lifetime supply of TOXIC magazines?

HAPPY HIPPO ⬣
Don't you just hate it when you are photobombed? HE'S BEHIND YOU MATE!

IS THIS MY BEST SIDE?

HELLOOO!

FUNNY FROG ⬣
Kermit's brother just looks relieved he doesn't have to deal with Miss Piggy!

DELIRIOUS DEER ◔
Q. What do you call a deer with one eye? A. No idea! This fella LOVES that joke!

GRINNING GORILLA ◔
We don't know what this chap is so chuffed about – he needs a trip to the dentist!

SNIGGERING SEAL ◔
Spending all day lounging on a beach makes you THIS happy? Sounds a bit fishy!

HILARIOUS HORSE ◔
Is this pony laughing his socks off or just feeling a little hoarse? Geddit? LOL!

DELIGHTED DOG ◔
This cheerful canine is clearly having A BALL! But who did he nick it from?

BATMAN
WORDSEARCH!

Can you capture 10 Bat-related words?

THIS IS SUPER TRICKY!

```
B V S H E A M K I C S N S E O
A E U G O T H A M C I T Y F A
T T T E P O E E R L G T I R L
C N I R Y E O C B V S P D N E
A R L W A S R O T W E V E A J
V N I S L P G H E R N L R T O
E N T O F N R B E I O T M E K
Y F Y D R N H E B R N E A N E
O U B E E E U O T A O I N A R
A H E O D U R T O E T H I B O
P G L D E R N N N I P M M T A
L N T E I E I I T L Y H A T I
T T O R H I R T N T E S M N N
G O R D O N I T R U E S F R P
J B R U C E W A Y N E O S E A
```

TICK OFF EVERY ONE YOU FIND!

- ■ BATCAVE
- ■ BRUCE WAYNE
- ■ ALFRED
- ■ BATMAN
- ■ BANE
- ■ GOTHAM CITY
- ■ GORDON
- ■ JOKER
- ■ ROBIN
- ■ UTILITY BELT

JUST FOR FUN!

DINO

Who'd win in a battle between these two?

REX-CELLENT!

DON'T CALL ME A FOSSIL!

T-REX! V

DINO FACT!
The T-Rex's teeth measured a whopping 30cm long and were shaped like a banana!

GET THE HEADS UP!

HEIGHT: 4 metres! (Roughly two and a half grown-ups stood head-to-toe).

SPEED: 24.85mph. Despite its humongous size, this dino was frighteningly quick too! RUN!

WEIGHT: 7 tonnes. That's nearly as much as a bus!

DIET: It fed on other dinos!

VISION: Hawk-like eyes meant catching prey was never hard!

WEAKNESSES: The two front arms were almost useless!

STRENGTHS: Its huge jaw meant only a few bites were needed to inflict damage!

✔ ❮❮❮❮❮ WHO WINS

WARS

STEGO-GO-GO!

YOU'RE A LAZY BONES

S STEGOSAURUS!

GET THE HEADS UP!

HEIGHT: 3.7 metres! (Roughly two grown-ups stood head-to-toe). Stego's were also a massive 9 metres long!

SPEED: 3.73mph. Not fast but masters of close combat!

WEIGHT: 3 tonnes. That's twice as heavy as a car!

DIET: They were big veggies!

VISION: Small heads meant poor vision and small brains!

WEAKNESSES: They relied on their size and power!

STRENGTHS: The spiked tail gave it a huge advantage over potential predators! SNEAKY!

DINO FACT!
The Stego's superb sense of smell meant they could detect any predators from afar!

OU DECIDE! >>> >>> ✓

SKYLANDERS

We've covered all the games for you to become an expert!

1 In Giants, check all areas on the Dread Yacht – you might find some hidden treasure! WOW!

2 Eruptor's fierce battle cries include "I came, I saw, I burned!" HOT!

3 Auric sells Lock Puzzle keys in his stores in Giants that allow you to skip past any Lock Puzzle you wish. That's why we LOVE HIM!

4 Skystones players like to use their stones in a certain way in Giants. Keep on going against the same player until you find their unique strategy and discover how to defeat them. CRAFTY!

AIR FORCE!

I'M REALLY HOT STUFF!

ALL FIRED UP!

5 Beating the game in Giants will unlock a new mode – NIGHTMARE! Be careful though as once you select this difficulty, you won't be able to change to an easier mode mid-game. BOO!

6 Trouble defeating Drill-X? Use Skylanders with large area-of-effect attacks to hit multiple sections of his drill! SIMPLE!

7 D. Riveter attacks friends and foes alike in Giants. Use this to your advantage when he's part of the mix to beat him! CLEVER!

ESSENTIAL FACTS

YOU TWIT OF FURY!

HE'S GOT SONIC WIND!

8 Arkeyan Crackler's clones look exactly like him, but move very differently. Spot the difference and you'll find him! GOTCHA!

9 **Heroic Challenges** are a great way to level up in any game. You can collect some extra buffs too. How cool is that?!

GUN SLINGER!

10 Lightning Rod's species is Storm Giant although he is not actually a giant! MASSIVE LIAR!

11 Need more hats? Then find Patterson's brother Hatterson on the Dread Yacht in Giants after collecting the Legendary Ship Part known as the Dragon Engine!

12 Having trouble winning Skystones? Auric can sell you some new Stones and special cheats so you can win any game. BRILL!

13 Play Skystones with characters you meet multiple times and you can collect both extra Skystones and more gold!

SKYLANDERS ESSENTIAL FACTS

14 Light Core Skylanders become smart bombs when they are placed on the Portal of Power, but only once per level. Use this when you're fighting big groups of enemies and win!

15 Ninjini is the only female Giant and she's also the only Giant that doesn't move boulders!

17 As well as ground-breaking new figures, the Swap-Force also introduced special characters that could jump, for the first time ever! COOL!

18 When Drobot's not hunting for Kaos, he relaxes by playing a game of chess against himself!

IRON GIANT!

16 The **Level Cap** has been raised from 10 in Spyro's Adventure, to 15 in Giants and then 20 in Swap Force! WOW!

I AM SOOO PRETTY!

ALL FIRED UP!

19 Bouncer is the one and only Giant to have a legendary version!

20 The Gold Prism Break figure is the rarest Skylander figure ever! Activision's staff were given some in 2012 and told to keep them until they left their job!

21 One of the very first Skylanders created as a figure was Bash from Skylanders Spyro's Adventure. He was initially called Rock Dragon before they decided to change his name!

22 The little-known Cyclops Snail was one of the first Skylanders ever. But his character evolved so much they scrapped him altogether! SORRY!

FUN TOWN!

26 Cutthroat Carnival is the last known place in **Skylands** you could get a churro. It's all thanks to Blobber's stupidity!

23 If you hold a Stealth Elf under a light, her eyes and daggers glow in the dark! COOL!

DEMON DRINK!

27 Auric has some great things for sale in his shop. However, at first we'd recommend spending gold on some Skylanders' upgrades from Persephone. You'll soon see why!

30 All Skylanders have individual quests. To find them go into the Skylander Info menu, select Quests and start exploring!

28 You'll find a hidden Earth area in the Arkeyan Armory level in Spyro's Adventure by taking an Earth Skylander and destroying the stone barrier around it! SNEAKY!

24 Series 2 Skylanders have an extra Wow Pow, which is devastating. Save up gold to get it!

25 Build Sprocket's turrets early in Giants! You don't get the chance to do it in the heat of a battle!

29 The most watched Skylanders video of all time is the official Giants trailer. Incredibly, the footgage has had over 12 million views! AMAZING!

NINJA SKUNK!

37

SKYLANDERS ESSENTIAL FACTS

31 The Nintendo 3DS version of Swap-Force was the first handheld version To include voice acting! SAY WHAT?!

32 To make quick cash, use the Sky Diamond magic item in Swap Force when you attack the training dummies. With luck, you can rack up 1,500 coins or more!

33 Freeze a bad guy if he's on a ledge AND THEN hammer him with Crusher! They'll have no chance!

MIND MAGIC!

34 Master Eon believes he can fully predict what choices people will make just by watching them closely. FREAKY!

35 ShroomBoom is great for hitting nasties hanging out on ledges. Just throw up your mushroom barrier and lob missiles from behind the ring. INCOMING!

36 There's a staggering 256 combinations to try out with all the Swap-Force characters! WOW!

37 Evil Kaos was born a Prince but was so bald, ugly and smelly that his father disowned him! NICE!

38 Enchanted Swap-Force figures such as Hoot Loop actually change colour when they are left in the sunlight! TAN-TASTIC!

BIRD BRAINS!

CRUSH HOUR!

I HATE SHOES!

SEA LORD!

39 **Wash Buckler ▶ was the first EVER Swap Force character to be seen in the trailer! AHOY!**

40 It's tricky to get behind Blaze Brewer in Giants, but if you focus attacks on his tank it will explode and hurl him out the level. SEE YA!

41 Chill's blades are no use against a gang of tough guys. So use her ice walls to freeze the enemy and then call in the Narwhal!

43 If your mate has a hat that you want just put it on one of your own Skylanders. That way, it'll be there when you get home!

44 In Swap-Force, treasure resets every time you visit Woodburrow. Also remember to check the Mushroom Staircase for extra loot all the way up! KA-CHING!

42 **The Wilkin were Kaos's toys, until he found he could make them come alive! COOL!**

45 Swarm is better in the air in Giants. Fly when you enter combat and you can sting foes sneaking up behind you! Plus, you can turn into a huge swarm of bees and escape! BRILLIANT!

MY BREATH STINKS!

TOXIC PUZZLES!

Have a go at these puzzles!

GO ON, PULL MY FINGER!

1 EON'S ELEMENTS!

Can you work out which order the Skylanders elements go in?

GOOD LUCK PORTAL MASTERS!

THE CODE IS:

1	2	3	4
5	6	7	8

FIRE — Must not be next to Water

TECH — Is in between Water and Life

AIR — Should be placed in fifth

WATER — Water must go first

MAGIC — Goes next to Fire

EARTH — Comes straight after Magic

UNDEAD — Must touch Life

LIFE — Must not go at the end

2 STARS IN THEIR CARS!

Blimey who are this lot? Can you guess which celebs are behind the wheel?

A ....

B ....

C ....

D ....

48

3 STARKS SPARKS!

Iron Man has blown up some famous landmarks! Can you guess them all?

BUT I'M A GOOD GUY!

MASSIVE CLOCK!

EGYPTIAN SHAPES!

NEW YORK GIANT!

HOME OF FOOTBALL!

A ....

B ....

C ....

D ....

ANSWERS ON PAGE 64!

4 CANDY CRUSH!

We've filled a jar full of sweets. How many of each one can you spot?

5 MINIFIGURE MIX!

Five LEGO minifigures have been combined to make one. Name them!

THIS IS NOT A GOOD LOOK!

CHEESE!

MONKEY NUT!

This black macaque monkey snapped a cheeky selfie when a photographer left his camera unguarded nearby! Judging by these efforts he should take it up professionally - or be a fashion model. Nice teeth mate!

Picture: Caters

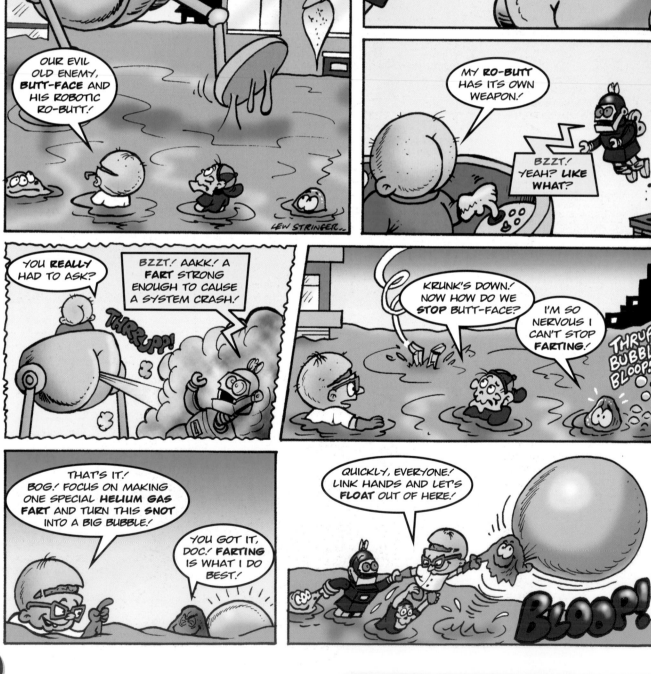

★★ Funniest ★★
YouTube FAILS!

These clips will have you cracking up!

ROCKIN' HORSE!

Word is that **Doc Shock** is hoping to add this horse to Team Toxic. Not even Captain Gross can produce **bottom burps** like this one!

You Tube Search | Horse Passing Gas | 🔍

WHAT A MISS-TAKE!

This football team might play in Liverpool red, but they **shoot like garbage** rather than Luis Suarez! Aim for the **ONION BAG!**

You Tube Search | How did they not score! | 🔍

TROUBLE ESCALATING!

Do not try this at home or your mum will go absolutely berserk! Plus, you'll end up with a very **sore bum** like this lad as well! OUCH!

You Tube Search | Escalator Sliding Split Fail | 🔍

CHIP & FAIL!

DON'T YOU SQUEAK A WORD!

Is this chipmunk an **evil genius** in disguise? Or just the **funniest rodent** on the planet? We reckon it's a combination of the two!

You Tube Search | Dramatic Chipmunk | 🔍

THIS IS HARDER THAN IT LOOKS.!

FALL GUY!

This chap thinks he is super cool – shame it's all about to go **horribly wrong**. Here's a clue mate – Hip Hop and treadmills DON'T MIX!

YouTube Search **Hip Hop Treadmill Fail** 🔍

NOT SO SUPER!

Why can't you ever find a **shopping trolley** in the supermarket? Because this driver has lost them all! Better get a bigger basket!

YouTube Search **Massive Shopping Cart Fail** 🔍

LAND AHOY!

Amazingly, the man driving this boat is **paid to do this** so that the ship can be broken up and recycled. We want that job **NOW!**

YouTube Search **Final destination: Ferry crashes** 🔍

PAIN IN THE NECK!

This **friendly giraffe** is called Perdy. Judging by the way he hangs around the food stalls, maybe he should change his name to 'Hungry'!

YouTube Search **Perdy Walking across restaurant** 🔍

SNOW JOKE!

Guess what happens when you attempt to **dig snow off your roof?** That's right: a homemade **avalanche!** WHITE ON TIME!

YouTube Search **Guy cleans snow off the roof** 🔍

HARE RAISING!

WHAT THE...?

Surely, this has got to be the **least scary animal swarm** on the planet. That's unless baby hamsters swarm too! **NO WAY!**

YouTube Search **Japanese Rabbit Attack** 🔍

DISNEY INFINITY!

It's the most awesome Disney world ever!

INCREDIBLE SET! ▶
A completely new film ending sees Syndrome unleash chaos on the Metro Building! RUN!

CRYSTAL CLEAR! ▶
Crystal figures earn totally sick powers like Lightning McQueen's super boost! BOOM!

MY ARM IS HUGE!

SCARE BULLIES! ◆
Fear Tech bullies will flee in the Monsters Uni set if you knock them down and roar!

OI! BUZZ OFF!

HEROES UNITE! ◆
Anything in the entire Disney stable, from Cars to Toy Story, can be in the game! SICK!

I HAVE TEETH LIKE A *SHARK*?

MONSTERS!

GO FIGURE! ◆
There are now loads of character figures to collect – and plenty more planned!

SUPER BAD! ◆
Walk a character off a ledge 40 times and you'll unlock a super secret achievement!

BOX OF TRICKS! ◆
You can build your own world in Toy Box mode or use a cool prebuilt Disney one!

WHY ARE OUR GUNS RED?

CHARMED LIFE! ◆
Find five bone charm locations in the Lone Ranger Play Set and you can fly as a crow!

10 REASONS WE LOVE...
MARIO

The Nintendo legend just keeps getting cooler!

1 HE'S ANCIENT! ⬇
The god of gaming has appeared in over 200 games since he first appeared in 1981! THAT'S A WORKLOAD!

WORLD 1-3   TIME 291

OLD SCHOOL!

2 EPIC POWER-UPS!
From giant mushrooms to chucking fireballs, right up to his new catsuit, Mario is one tough customer!

3 LOTS OF CHOICE! ⬇
If you don't like platform games, Mazza's been in puzzlers, racers and FIGHTING games. BASH!

4 HIS 'TACHE! ⬆
In his first game Mario was given face-fuzz so you could tell the difference between his nose and chin!

I'M-A THE BEST-A!

MARIO KART!

5 HE CAN RACE! ⬦
The Mario Kart games are totally sick! The latest one, Mario Kart 8, is the best of the lot! ZOOM!

6 THE MUSIC ⬇
The classic Mario Brothers tunes get stuck in your head as soon as you listen to them! HARMONY!

7 LOADS OF FOES!
As well as Bowser, Mario has to fight off crazy foes like Goomba, Koopa Troopa and Bullet Bill!

ACE TUNES!

8 HE'S MOBILE!
As well as playing Mario games at home on the Wii U, there's loads of great 3DS games to play too! 1-UP!

9 HIS MATES! ⬦
He's got back-up – in the form of Luigi, Toad and Princess Peach, who keeps getting kidnapped! BOO!

10 FOOTY GAME! ⬦
Mazza was more like Mario BALOTELLI in the cool Super Mario Strikers game on the Wii! GOALAZIO!

© 2014 Nintendo Co. Ltd

INVASION!
Where weird worlds collide!

WHAT TO DO!

Team Toxic have used their mega-powers to sneak into the amazing world of Disney Infinity! The only way to kick them out is to find all 10 mini-images of Doc Shock, Bog, Kid Zombie, Krunk and Sludge! Can you do it?

NO CHANCE!

JUST FOR FUN!

WE'VE BEEN INVADED!

WHEN CELEBS LOOK LIKE CRAZY ANIMALS!

ANT MCPARTLIN

YAWNING MONKEY

BRITNEY SPEARS

BONKERS BABOON

RONALDO

GURNING GORILLA

DAVID LUIZ

PERMED POOCH

GARETH BALE

MOUTHY MONKEY

HARRY STYLES

FRIGHTENED FISH

KRISTEN STEWART

GRUMPY CAT

LOUIS TOMLINSON

BIG CHEEKED APE

Pictures: Getty Images, Alamy-ImageCollect, istockphoto.com, Shutterstock, 123RF, Rex, Wenn, Eroteme, Barcroft Media, Golf Photo, NaturePL.com, Photoshot

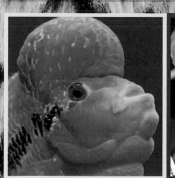

GARY BARLOW

CHEEKY MONKEY

BROTHERS?

NICKI MINAJ **CRAZY GOLDFISH**

PRINCE HARRY **YODELING CHIMP**

PRINCE WILLIAM **CHUCKLING HORSE**

CHRIS HEMSWORTH **HAIRY HOUND**

PUZZLE ANSWERS

PAGE 17 — CHIMA SPOT THE DIFFERENCE!

PAGE 50 — FIFA SPOT THE DIFFERENCE!

PAGE 24-25 — MARIO KART INVASION!

PAGE 48-49 — TOXIC PUZZLES!

1. EON'S ELEMENTS!

2. STARS IN THEIR CARS!
A. JOHNNY DEPP
B. ANT AND DEC
C. WAYNE ROONEY
D. THE ROCK

3. STARKS SPARKS!
A. BIG BEN
B. PYRAMIDS
C. EMPIRE STATE BUILDING
D. WEMBLEY

4. CANDY CRUSH!
6
7
4
8
5
8

5. MINIFIGURE MIX!
A. GOLDEN NINJA
B. IRON MAN
C. MR. GOLD
D. SUPERMAN

PAGE 27 — POKEMON MAZE!

PAGE 31 — BATMAN WORDSEARCH!

```
B V S H E A M K I C S N S E O
A E U G O T H A M C I T Y F A
T T T E P O E E R L G T I R L
C N I R V E O C B V S P D N E
A R L W A S R O T W E V E A J
V N I S L P G H E R N L R T O
E N T O F N R B E I O T M E K
Y F V D R N H E B R N E A N E
O U B E E E U O T A O I N A R
A H E O D U R T O E T H I B O
P G L D E R N N N I P M M T A
L N T E I E I I T L Y H A T I
T T O R H I R T N T E S M N N
G O R D O N I T R U E S F R P
J B R U C E W A Y N E O S E A
```

PAGE 60-61 — DISNEY INFINITY INVASION!

SPOT 'EM!